EXPLORE ECOSYSTEMS

IN A TREE

SARAH RIDLEY

WAYLAND

First published in Great Britain in 2022
by Wayland

Editor: Amy Pimperton
Designer: Lisa Peacock
Picture researchers: Diana Morris, Sarah Ridley

ISBN: 978 1 5263 2247 0 (hardback); 978 1 5263 2248 7 (paperback)

Printed and bound in China

Wayland, an imprint of
Hachette Children's Group
Part of Hodder and Stoughton
Carmelite House
50 Victoria Embankment
London EC4Y 0DZ
An Hachette UK Company
www.hachette.co.uk
www.hachettechildrens.co.uk

MIX
Paper from
responsible sources
FSC
www.fsc.org   FSC® C104740

Picture acknowledgements:
Nature PL: Andrew Cooper 26; Silvia Reiche 11b; Andy Sands 11t, 19b; Kim Taylor 13t, 21b;
Duncan Usher 22l; Mike Wilkes 16; Solvin Zankl 23t.
Shutterstock: Bildagentur Zoonar GmbH 24c; Aleksander Bolbot 3, 29t; Neil Bromhall 29b;
Lubos Chlubny 18b; Digoarpi 6bl; Dja65 5t; FJAH 18t; Martin Fowler 20t, 32; Thijs de Graaf 10;
Simon Groewe 21t; Pascal Halder 17t; Joachim Heller 30b; Miroslav Hlavko 27t;
Inspiring Moments 14-15b; Aleksey Karpenko cover bl; Kichigin 7t; D Kucharski, K Kucharska 27b;
Maryna Lipatova 15t; Ivan Marjanovic 6br; Maksim Miasnikou 4b; Passing By 28; Allen Paul
Photography 4t; Place-to-be 30t; Ondrej Prosicky cover br; Javier Ramil 22r; Mike Russel 20b;
SakSa cover t; Self-taught 24b; Smileus 1t, 8bl; Sandra Standbridge 14l; Stanislavskyi 17b;
Alex Stemmers 9t; Deborah Waters 7b; Paul Alexander Watkins 5b;YK 1b, 12, 13; Lukas Zdrazil 25r.

Every attempt has been made to clear copyright. Should there be any
inadvertent omission please apply to the publisher for rectification.

Contents

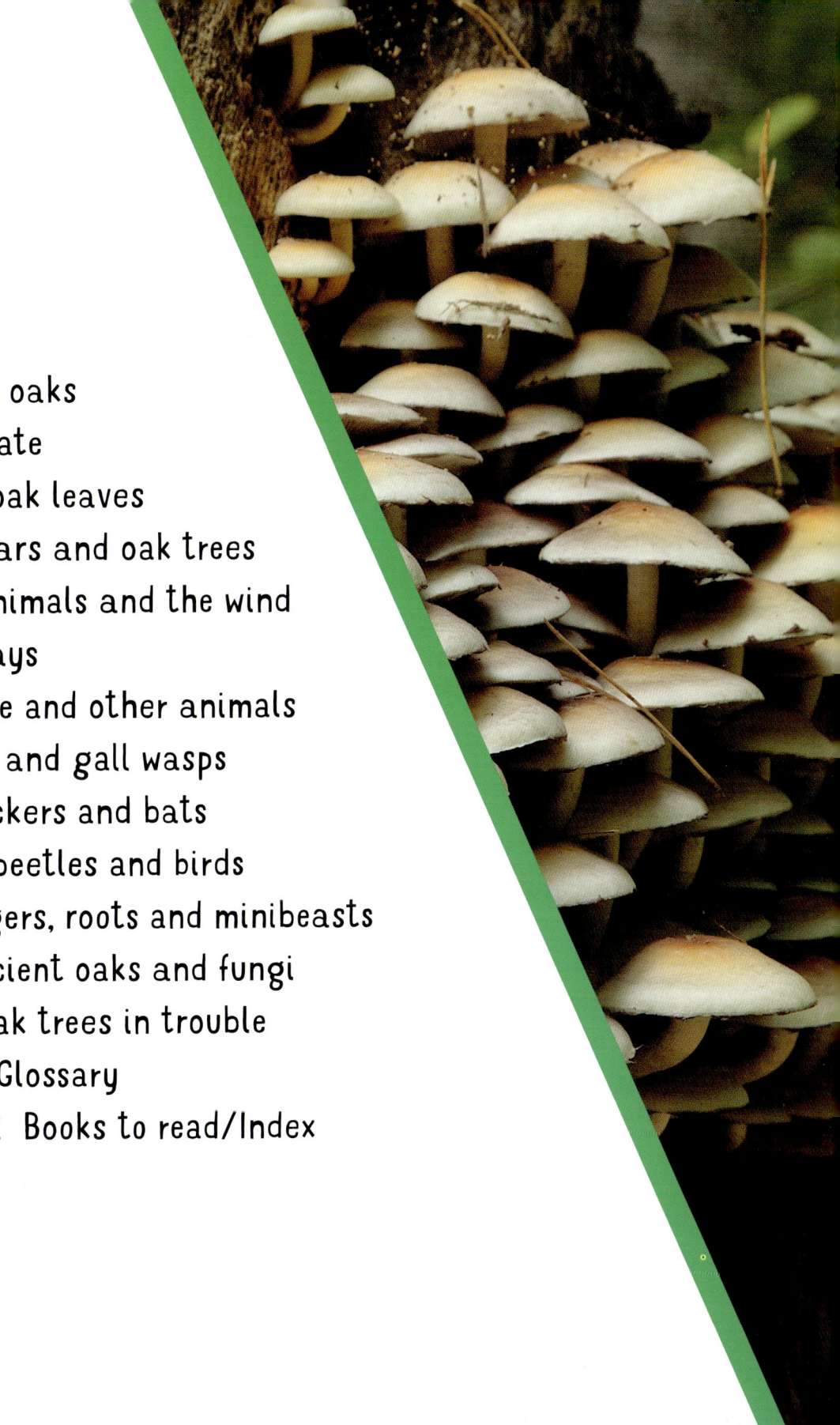

A tree ecosystem is all the living things and non-living things in a tree, and the different ways they are connected to each other.

Oak tree

An oak tree and soil

An oak tree stands tall in the summer sunshine.
Oak trees grow in many places around the world.

Oak trees offer shelter and food to thousands of living things,
including spiders and birds. All the different ways these living
things are connected to each other and to non-living things,
such as soil and water, form a small ecosystem.

An oak tree ecosystem needs one thing more than any other: soil. Tree roots grow through the soil, covering an area wider than the tree's widest branches.

The roots hold the tree in place and soak up oxygen, water and nutrients. These pass along the roots and up the trunk to keep the tree alive.

Oak tree roots

Roots need soil to hold the tree steady and provide it with what it needs to stay alive.

Tawny owl

Marbled orb-weaver spider

Fungi, roots and other oaks

In the summer and autumn, penny buns, or ceps, grow out of the ground near trees, including oaks.

Penny buns are the fruiting bodies – or mushrooms – of a fungus. Snails, slugs and mice eat them.

Penny buns

Snail

Thread-like fungi

Thread-like fungi

Underground, different types of thread-like fungus grow around and inside oak roots. In return for some of the tree's sugary sap, the fungi bring special nutrients into the roots and help them soak up water.

These helpful fungi are part of a vast network called the wood wide web. Trees including oaks use the wood wide web to support each other by sharing nutrients and water with young, old or ill trees.

Oak woodland

Oak trees need helpful fungi for healthy growth and to support the wood wide web.

Leaves and the climate

Sunlight streams through the leaves and branches of an oak tree. Its fresh green leaves unfurled when the weather warmed up in spring.

Oak tree in sunlight

Tree leaves take carbon dioxide from the air to make food for the tree and release oxygen for animals to breathe.

Oak leaf

Leaves are a tree's food factories. They use the Sun's energy to turn carbon dioxide, water and nutrients into sugary food for the tree. This process, called photosynthesis, releases oxygen into the air. All animals, including humans, breathe in oxygen to stay alive.

A tree stores carbon dioxide in its trunk, branches and roots for as long as it lives. In this way, all trees – including oaks – are helping to slow down climate change by removing carbon dioxide – one of the greenhouse gases – from Earth's atmosphere.

Owlet moth caterpillar

Caterpillars and oak leaves

Soon after the green leaves open out, caterpillars start to munch them. They have hatched from eggs laid by moths and butterflies.

The caterpillars eat and eat, growing bigger and bigger until it is time to turn into an adult moth or butterfly. Usually, an oak tree can cope with lots of caterpillars eating its leaves as it has so many.

Some sorts of caterpillar eat only oak leaves. The female hairstreak butterfly lays her eggs close to oak leaf buds high in the treetops. The following spring, her caterpillars hatch and eat oak flower buds and leaves. They rest during the day and munch at night to avoid predators.

Female purple hairstreak butterfly

Many butterflies and moths need oak leaves as they are the perfect habitat for their caterpillars.

Oak leaf buds

Purple hairstreak butterfly egg (white)

11

Chicks, caterpillars and oak trees

Birds fly to and from oak trees in spring. They are searching among the leaves for caterpillars to take back to their chicks.

Blue tit with caterpillars

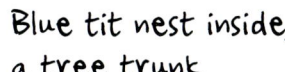

Blue tit nest inside a tree trunk

Back at the nest, hungry chicks wait with open beaks. The parent birds drop caterpillars and other insects into their chicks' mouths. Blue tit and great tit chicks need to eat about a hundred caterpillars each per day. That's a lot of caterpillars for their parents to find.

Birds help oak trees by feeding caterpillars that eat oak leaves to their chicks. Oak trees provide places for birds to build nests.

Spotted flycatcher nest

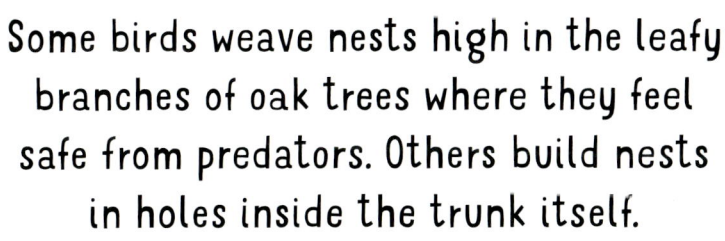

Some birds weave nests high in the leafy branches of oak trees where they feel safe from predators. Others build nests in holes inside the trunk itself.

Oak flowers, animals and the wind

Squirrels scamper along the branches of oak trees in spring.
They are looking for catkins to eat.

Grey squirrel

The dangly catkins are an oak tree's male flowers. They are covered in pollen, a tasty food for many insects. Small birds come to the tree in search of insects, and larger birds hunt those small birds.

The wind carries male oak pollen to the tiny female flowers of oak trees nearby. In the same way, pollen from another oak tree will reach this oak tree's female flowers, allowing them to make acorns, which squirrels love to eat.

Oak catkins

Acorns

Oak flowers are food for several animals. Oak trees need the non-living wind to make acorns.

15

Acorns and jays

In the autumn, acorns fall from oak trees.

Jays pick acorns up and pluck them from branches.
The birds are in a hurry as many other animals eat acorns, too.

Eurasian jay

A jay can carry up to nine acorns in a pouch inside its throat, and one more acorn in its beak. It flies off to hide the acorns in the ground or in holes in trees. Back and forth it flies, storing thousands of acorns for the long winter months ahead.

Eurasian jay

The jay remembers where it has hidden its acorns and returns to eat them. However, it usually only eats about a quarter of the acorns it hides. Some of the buried acorns will grow into oak seedlings the following spring.

Oak seedling

Jays help to spread an oak tree's seeds far from the parent tree by burying acorns to eat later.

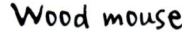
Wood mouse

Roe deer

Acorns, mice and other animals

At night, wood mice leave their underground burrows to search for food. In autumn, they eat acorns as well as other seeds.

Wood mice are not the only animals to eat acorns. Deer, badgers, squirrels, wild boars, birds and some insects all enjoy an acorn feast.

The oak weevil does not eat acorns, but its larvae do. A female oak weevil uses her long snout to bore a hole in several acorns in the early summer. She lays an egg or two inside each hole and, when they hatch, the larvae eat their acorn home. Once the acorns drop to the ground, the larvae tunnel out and continue growing in the soil.

Female oak weevil

Many animals depend on acorns as food for themselves or their young.

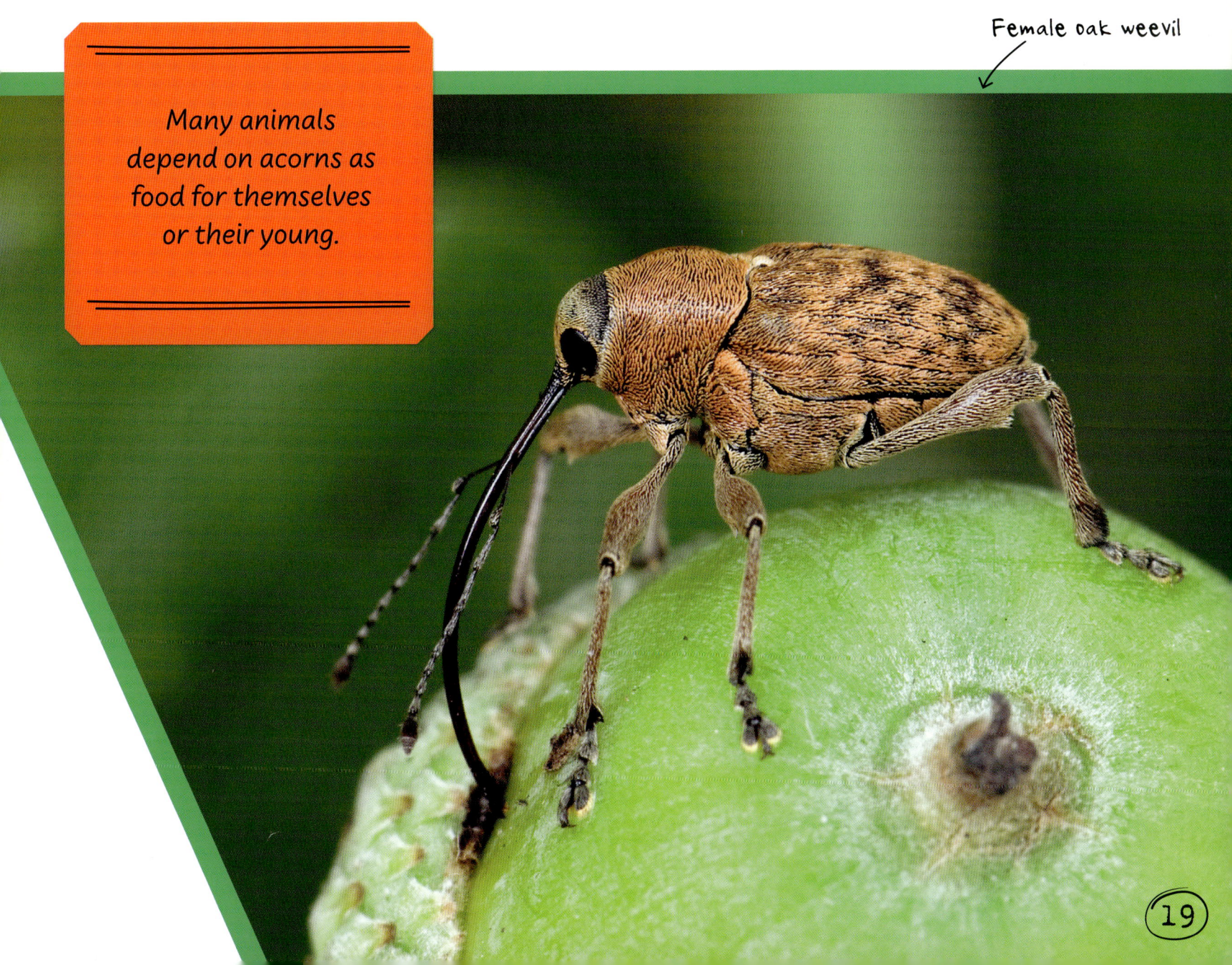

Oak galls and gall wasps

Look up into an oak tree and you may spot oak galls. They are home to the young of oak gall wasps.

Hundreds of different sorts of gall wasp live around the world and many of them have a close relationship with oak trees.

Oak marble galls

Oak knopper gall

Each species of wasp creates a different oak gall. The odd shape on this acorn contains several gall wasp larvae ...

Silk button galls

... and each of these tiny 'button' shapes contains a single gall wasp larva.

Gall wasp emerged from gall

This gall wasp's life started after its mother laid an egg inside a leaf bud. Next, she injected a special liquid into the bud to make it grow extra material around her egg. This formed an oak gall. Safe inside, the larva hatched and grew until it changed into an adult and pulled itself out of its oak gall home.

Many sorts of gall wasp use oak trees to provide homes for their young.

Woodpeckers and bats

Woodpeckers make nests in oaks and other trees. They use their sharp beaks to hollow out a nest hole to keep their chicks safe.

A woodpecker's sharp beak is also useful for finding food. It hammers its beak into bark and uses its long tongue to pull out beetle larvae living in the wood. The bird helps the tree by eating the larvae that are munching away on its wood.

Woodpecker, larva and chick

Greater spotted woodpecker

Pipistrelle bat

Once a woodpecker family has finished with a nest hole, bats sometimes move in. They sleep during the day and hunt for food at night. When autumn turns to winter, sleep takes over. If the hole is deep enough, it will be the perfect place for bats to hibernate.

By making nest holes in oak trees, woodpeckers also create homes for bats.

Bark, beetles and birds

As it grows, an oak tree's bark changes from smooth to rough. The bark develops deep cracks, which provide shelter for many different minibeasts, including beetles.

Mosses and plant-like living things called lichen make their homes on the bark. Birds use lichen and moss as building material for their nests.

Longhorn beetle

Lichen

Cup lichen and moss

Treecreeper

Some beetles lay their eggs inside deep cracks in the bark. When the larvae hatch, they eat into the wood, creating tunnels. Most beetle larvae feed on dead or dying parts of the tree rather than healthy living wood.

Beetles and their larvae attract predators including birds. A treecreeper uses its sharp curved beak to hunt for beetles and other insects hiding in the bark.

Bark provides the perfect habitat for lichen, moss, beetles, their larvae and many other insects, attracting birds in search of food.

25

Badgers, roots and minibeasts

Badger cubs play in their underground home, safe among the roots of an oak tree.

Badgers live in family groups in a home called a sett. They work together to dig out underground tunnels connected to chambers.

In the evening, badgers come out of their sett to hunt for food. They use their excellent sense of smell to find fruits, and the small animals and minibeasts that live among fallen leaves and twigs.

Earthworms are a badger's favourite food. It digs them out of the ground and uses its sharp claws to break open deadwood to find earthworms living inside.

Badger hunting for food

Oak tree roots and fallen leaves provide a home and hunting ground for badgers.

Earthworm

Ancient oaks and fungi

Once an oak is 400 years old, it is called an ancient oak. It will continue to grow for hundreds of years.

Gradually branches fall off. Parts of the tree start to die to form deadwood. The fallen branches and deadwood become a perfect habitat for living things, including fungi.

Ancient oak

Many species of fungus live on oak deadwood. They are decomposers, helping to break down the deadwood and release the nutrients locked up inside. The fungi help to return nutrients to the soil.

Fungi on deadwood

Fungi break down deadwood and recycle its nutrients into the soil where it can be reused by plants, including oak trees.

By breaking down deadwood, fallen branches and leaves, fungi and other decomposers help clean up dead stuff. The nutrients they return to the soil help oak seedlings and their parent trees grow tall and strong.

Oak seedling

oak trees in trouble

All around the world, different species of oak are in danger from plant diseases, pests, climate change and the action of people.

One pest that is spreading around Europe is the oak processionary moth and its caterpillars. The caterpillars follow each other nose-to-tail and eat a huge number of leaves, making the tree grow weak. Keep away from these caterpillars as they can make you feel ill.

Oak processionary moth caterpillars

The longer an oak tree lives, the greater the variety of living things it supports. As oak trees grow slowly, if people chop them down to build roads or buildings it will take hundreds of years for other oak trees to replace them.

Chopped down oak tree

This book has explored some of the connections between the living and non-living things in an oak tree ecosystem. We need to take care of oak trees and all the life they support in this precious ecosystem, so that the connections between these groups are not broken.

Glossary

acorn the fruit (containing the seed) of an oak tree

atmosphere the gases surrounding Earth

carbon dioxide a gas plants use to make their food; a gas breathed out by animals

climate change a change in the normal weather around the world

deadwood parts of a tree that are dead

decomposer a living thing that helps break down dead stuff into tiny bits

ecosystem a community of living things and their environment

fungi living things that usually feed on dead material

greenhouse gas one of the gases, including carbon dioxide, which is building up in Earth's atmosphere, leading to climate change

habitat the usual home of a living thing

hibernate to spend the winter asleep

larvae the young of insects, fish and some other animals

moss a green plant with tiny leaves and no flowers

nutrient a substance that helps plants and animals to live and grow

oxygen the gas that all animals need to breathe to stay alive

pest an animal that harms plants

photosynthesis the process plants use to make their own food using carbon dioxide, water, nutrients and energy from sunlight

pollen a fine powder made by the male part of a flower

predator an animal that hunts and eats other animals

recycle to break down and reuse materials

seed the small hard part of a plant from which a new plant grows

seedling a young plant

snout a long nose

species a kind of living thing, such as a grey squirrel

Books to read

Follow the Food Chain (series)
by Sarah Ridley (Wayland, 2021)

The Big Picture: Living Habitats
by Jon Richards and illustrated by
Josy Bloggs (Franklin Watts, 2021)

The Great Nature Hunt: Trees
by Clare Hibbert (Franklin Watts, 2019)

Index